P9-EED-748

First published in Switzerland under the title *Rumpelstilzchen*

First published in the United States, Great Britain, Canada, Australia, and New Zealand in 1993 by North-South Books, an imprint of Nord-Süd Verlag AG, Gossau Zürich, Switzerland.
First paperback edition published in 1996.

Distributed in the United States by North-South Books Inc., New York.

Library of Congress Cataloging-in-Publication Data
Rumpelstilzchen (Grimm version). English
Rumpelstiltskin : a fairy tale / by the Brothers Grimm ;
illustrated by Bernadette Watts ; translated by Anthea Bell.
Summary: A strange little man helps the miller's daughter spin straw into gold for the king, on the condition that she will give him her first-born child.
[1. Fairy tales. 2. Folklore—Germany.] I. Grimm, Jacob, 1785-1863.
II. Grimm, Wilhelm, 1786-1859. III. Watts, Bernadette, ill.
IV. Bell, Anthea. V. Title.
PZ8.R89Wat 1993 92-31331
398.21—dc20 [E]

A CIP catalogue record for this book is available from The British Library.
ISBN 1-55858-617-2 (PAPERBACK)
1 3 5 7 9 PB 10 8 6 4 2
Printed in Belgium

For information about our books, and the authors and artists who create them, visit our web site:
http://www.northsouth.com

Rumpelstiltskin

A FAIRY TALE BY THE

Brothers Grimm

ILLUSTRATED BY

Bernadette Watts

TRANSLATED BY

Anthea Bell

North-South Books
NEW YORK

ONCE UPON A TIME there was a poor miller who had a beautiful daughter.

One day the miller happened to meet the king and, wanting to impress him, boasted, “I have a daughter who can spin straw into gold.”

“I like the sound of that!” said the king to the miller. “If your daughter is really as clever as you say, bring her to my castle tomorrow and I’ll put her to the test.”

When the girl arrived, the king took her into a room full of straw, gave her a bobbin and a spinning wheel, and said, "Now you must set to work. You can spin all night, but if you haven't spun this straw into gold by morning, you must die." And with these words, he locked the door of the room and left her alone inside.

The poor miller's daughter was at her wits' end. She had no idea how to spin straw into gold, and she was so frightened that she began to cry.

All of a sudden the door opened, and in came a strange little man.

"Good evening, miller's daughter," he said. "Why are you crying so bitterly?"

"Oh dear!" said the girl. "I have to spin this straw into gold by morning, and I don't know how."

"What will you give me to spin it for you?" asked the little man.

"I'll give you my necklace," said the girl.

The little man took the necklace and sat down at the spinning wheel. *Whirr, whirr, whirr*—it went around three times, and the bobbin was full. He fitted another bobbin to the wheel. It went *whirr, whirr, whirr* three times again, and the second bobbin was full. So he went on, and by morning all the straw had been spun and all the bobbins held pure gold.

At sunrise the king came into the room. When he saw the gold he was amazed, and very pleased, but the sight of all that gold made him greedier than ever.

He took the miller's daughter into a much larger room full of straw, and told her that if she valued her life, she must spin all the straw into gold in a single night.

Not knowing what to do, the poor girl burst into tears. Once again the door opened, and there stood the little man. "What will you give me to spin this straw into gold for you?" he asked.

"I'll give you the ring from my finger," said the girl.

The little man took the ring and set the spinning wheel whirring. By morning he had spun all the straw into bright gold.

The king was delighted when he set eyes on the gold, but he wanted still more, so he took the miller's daughter into an even bigger room full of straw.

"You must spin this straw into gold tonight, and if you do, I will marry you," he told her.

For though she's only a miller's daughter, he thought, I couldn't find a richer wife in the whole world.

When the girl was alone, the little man appeared for the third time. "What will you give me to spin this straw into gold for you?" he asked.

"I have nothing left to give," replied the girl.

"Then promise me your first child when you are queen."

Well, the girl thought, who knows what may happen yet? As she could see no other way out, she promised the little man her first child. In return, he spun the straw into gold.

In the morning, when the king came and found everything just as he had hoped, he married the girl. And so the miller's beautiful daughter became queen.

A year later she had a lovely little baby. She had quite forgotten about the little man. Then, one day, he suddenly appeared. "Now give me what you promised," he demanded.

The queen was horrified. She promised the little man all the riches of the kingdom if only he would let her keep her child, but the little man said, "No, I'd rather have a living creature than all the riches in the world."

Then the queen began to weep and wail so pitifully that the little man felt sorry for her. "I'll give you three days' grace," he said. "If you can find out what my name is within that time, then you may keep your child."

The queen spent the whole night thinking of all the names she had ever heard, and she sent a messenger out to search the kingdom far and wide for more names.

When the little man came next day, she tried every name she knew, beginning with Caspar, Melchior, and Balthazar, but each time the little man replied, "No, that's not my name."

On the second day she had inquiries made in the countryside near the castle, to find out what the local people were called, and she tried some very strange and unusual names when the little man came.

"Is your name by any chance Skinnyribs? Is your name Leg of Mutton? Maybe you're called Spindleshanks?"

But every time he said, "No, that's not my name."

On the third day the messenger came back. "I didn't find a single new name," he said. "But when I was coming to a high mountain, just as I reached the corner of the forest where fox and hare meet, I saw a little house with a fire burning outside, and a strange little man dancing in the firelight, hopping on one leg and crying:

'Today I brew, tomorrow I'll bake,
And then the queen's sweet child I'll take.
How glad I am she never will claim
That Rumpelstiltskin is my name!'"

How happy the queen was to hear that! Not long after, the little man came in.

"Well, my lady queen, what's my name?" he said.

"Is your name Jack?" she asked.

"No."

"Is your name John?"

"No."

"Then is your name by any chance Rumpelstiltskin?"

"The devil told you that, the devil told you that!" cried the little man angrily, and he stamped his right foot so hard that he sank into the ground up to his waist.

Then, in his rage, he seized his left foot in both hands and tore himself in two.